Peanut-Butter Pilgrims

YOUNG YEARLING BOOKS YOU WILL ENJOY:

The Pee Wee Scout Books by Judy Delton
COOKIES AND CRUTCHES
CAMP GHOST-AWAY
LUCKY DOG DAYS
BLUE SKIES, FRENCH FRIES
GRUMPY PUMPKINS
PEANUT-BUTTER PILGRIMS
A PEE WEE CHRISTMAS
THAT MUSHY STUFF
SPRING SPROUTS

YEARLING BOOKS/YOUNG YEARLINGS/YEARLING CLAS-SICS are designed especially to entertain and enlighten young people. Patricia Reilly Giff, consultant to this series, received the bachelor's degree from Mary-mount College. She holds the master's degree in history from St. John's University, and a Professional Diploma in Reading from Hofstra University. She was a teacher and reading consultant for many years, and is the author of numerous books for young readers.

For a complete listing of all Yearling titles, write to
Dell Readers Service, P.O. Box 1045,
South Holland, IL 60473.

Peanut-Butter Pilgrims

JUDY DELTON

Illustrated by Alan Tiegreen

A YOUNG YEARLING BOOK

For Beverly Vavoulis,
friend and scribe

Published by
Dell Publishing
a division of
The Bantam Doubleday Dell Publishing Group, Inc.
666 Fifth Avenue
New York, New York 10103

ISBN: 0-440-40066-X

Printed in the United States of America

November 1988

10 9 8 7 6

Contents

CHAPTER 1

In-and-Out Baskets

"My basket is too skinny," cried Molly Duff. "I'll only be able to get one can of vegetables in it!"

"That is because you are weaving it too tightly," said Mrs. Peters kindly. Mrs. Peters was the Pee Wee Scout leader.

The Pee Wee Scouts were busy weaving baskets. They would get a basket-weaving badge when they finished. Then they would fill the baskets with food for poor families on Thanksgiving.

"Watch me again," said Mrs. Peters.

In and out.

In and out.

Little strips of wood.

Between the little sticks that stood up in the basket.

"If you pull too hard, the basket will be small. Weave loosely between the sticks. We have to get lots of good food in the baskets for Thanksgiving dinners."

"Look at mine, Mrs. Peters!" called Rachel Meyers. Rachel waved her basket over her head.

Mrs. Peters took Rachel's basket. She held it up for the Scout troop to see.

"Mine is big," said Rachel proudly. "I can get lots of food in mine."

"It is a little too big, Rachel," Mrs. Peters said. "You have woven it so loosely that some of the food may fall through the sides."

Rachel looked as if she would cry. She didn't like it when something was wrong.

"Now, here, you see Roger's basket? His isn't too loose and it isn't too tight. It is just right to hold food for a Thanksgiving dinner." Mrs. Peters held up Roger White's basket.

"A turkey won't fit in," said Rachel, still hurt about her too-loose basket. "And you need a turkey for Thanksgiving."

"We won't put the turkeys in the baskets," said Mrs. Peters. "The turkeys will come from Mrs. Atkins's turkey farm. They have to be kept cold."

Molly looked at Roger White's basket. It was all finished. It was just right. It started small at the bottom, and got bigger toward the top. It would hold lots of food.

Molly sighed and began again.

In and out.

In and out she wove.

3

"Looser, looser," she whispered to herself.

Rachel was trying to squeeze hers together so she wouldn't have to weave it over.

Squeeze, squeeze, squeeze.

Scrunch, push, shove.

The basket stayed the same.

"You can't squeeze it," said Roger, laughing. "You have to take it apart. You have to do it over."

Rachel stuck her tongue out at Roger. She looked as if she didn't want to do it over. She wanted it to be perfect the first time.

"All right!" called Mrs. Peters. "Let's finish up now. Those who are through may put their baskets here on the table, and start to clean up the scraps."

Molly wished she were finished. She wished she were cleaning up scraps. Instead, she kept weaving.

In and out.

In and out.

Mrs. Peters was helping Rachel unweave her loose basket. Rachel began to weave again.

In and out.

In and out.

Just as Mrs. Peters said "Our time is up for today," Molly finished. Her basket was not skinny now. It was not too fat either. It looked just right to hold food.

Rachel's looked better too. It wasn't quite finished. So it was shorter than the other Scout baskets.

The Scouts scrambled after all the scraps of wood and wicker. Kevin Moe swept the floor. Tim Noon held the dustpan.

Then Mrs. Peters said, "These are wonderful baskets! Someone will feel good to get one on Thanksgiving Day."

Mrs. Peters called out names for the badges.

The basket-weaving badges.

"Tracy Barnes," she said.

Tracy went up and got her badge. Her nose was running. Tracy's nose was always running, thought Molly. It was because of allergies.

"Sonny Betz!" called Mrs. Peters. Sonny went up and got his badge. His basket was good. Sonny was artistic.

Patty and Kenny Baker, the twins, went up for their badges.

Then Rachel and Roger.

And Lisa Ronning and Mary Beth Kelly and Tim Noon.

Just when Molly thought Mrs. Peters had forgotten about her, she heard, "Molly Duff!"

Molly thanked Mrs. Peters for the badge, and pinned it on her blouse with her other badges.

It was fun to get a brand-new badge. All shiny and clean. She was proud to have so many badges for doing good deeds and helping people.

When they all had their badges, the Scouts helped Mrs. Peters put the food in the baskets.

"My mom sent this dog food," said Sonny.

"Dogs aren't poor!" shouted Roger. "Ho, ho! Sonny brought food for a poor dog!"

"There are lots of poor dogs," said Tim. "I see them sniffing around garbage cans."

"That's right," said Mrs. Peters. "There are homeless animals to think of. Dogs and cats. Some pets need food too."

Molly put a can of spinach in her basket. And some cranberries.

Kevin put in a jar of peanut butter.

"Who will eat peanut butter on Thanksgiving?" said Mary Beth.

"It's for after Thanksgiving," he said. "When the turkey and stuffing are gone."

"What's this?" said Tracy. She was waving a can without a label.

"Did someone bring cans without labels on them?" asked Mrs. Peters.

Mary Beth's face turned red. She raised her hand. "I did," she said. "My little sister tore off the labels."

Mrs. Peters said, "We will put just one unlabeled can in each basket. That way everyone will have one surprise for dinner!"

She always knows what to do, thought Molly.

When the baskets were filled, Mrs. Peters made some announcements. "I have some surprises too," she said.

The Scouts sat up tall.

They liked surprises.

"Is your baby here?" asked Sonny.

Everyone laughed. He should be able to see the baby isn't here, thought Molly. Mrs. Betz should tell Sonny about babies. Mrs. Peters was fatter than ever!

"No." Mrs. Peters laughed. "Not until

next month. My surprise is that we are going to go to visit a turkey farm next week. Mrs. Atkins has invited us to see her turkeys and learn how she raises them."

"Yeah!" The Pee Wees cheered.

"And my other surprise," Mrs. Peters went on, "is that we will give a small Thanksgiving play at the town hall. A pilgrim play."

The Pee Wees cheered again.

They loved plays.

They loved to dress up.

All but Molly. I can't act, she thought. Being in a play didn't feel like a good surprise to Molly. It felt like a lot of hard work. Scary too.

"I love Thanksgiving," said Lisa. "Lots of turkey to eat."

Molly's mouth watered. She loved turkey. Turkey and cranberries and dressing and pumpkin pie. With whipped cream. And all the good smells in the house. Molly rubbed her stomach.

"I can't wait," she said. For the dinner, she thought, not the play.

The Scout meeting was over. The Pee Wees joined hands and said their Pee Wee Scout pledge. Then they sang their Pee Wee Scout song.

Now they would wait for next week. And their visit to Mrs. Atkins's turkey farm.

CHAPTER 2

Turkey Talk

"Take your time," called Mrs. Peters as the Pee Wees pushed to get on the bus. "We aren't going till everyone is on!"

Molly wanted to get a good seat. She and Mary Beth wanted to sit in the front so they would be the first ones to see the turkey farm. Roger and Sonny sat way in the back of the bus.

Mrs. Peters and Mrs. Betz sat in the middle. Mrs. Betz came along to help Mrs. Peters. To be sure no one got lost on the turkey farm.

It was Saturday. A long day stretched ahead. A perfect day to ride to the country.

The Pee Wees talked about Thanksgiving. And the turkeys. And the play at the town hall. They talked about school and vacation and their grandmas, who were coming from out of town.

Then they all sang "Over the River and Through the Woods." By that time they were at the turkey farm.

"I see them!" shouted Mary Beth. "I see the turkeys!"

Everyone ran to the windows on Mary Beth's side of the bus. Sure enough, far out in the field there were lots and lots of feathers. And bobbing heads. It looked like an ocean of white.

"Hello," said Mrs. Atkins when the Scouts tumbled off the bus. "Welcome to Atkins's turkey farm."

Mrs. Peters and Mrs. Betz shook hands

with Mrs. Atkins and introduced the Pee Wee Scouts.

"The turkeys are waiting for you," she said.

"Really?" said Sonny. "Do they know we are coming?"

The Scouts laughed.

"Actually, turkeys don't know much." Mrs. Atkins chuckled. "They just peck, peck, peck all day long."

Before they walked to the field, Mrs. Atkins told the Scouts about turkey farming. She told them what the turkeys ate, and how big they got, and when they were ready to go to market.

Then Mrs. Atkins led them out to the field.

"Why are there so many?" asked Tracy. "It looks like millions and millions of turkeys."

"Thanksgiving is coming," said Mrs. Atkins. "And next month is Christmas. Lots of people have turkey for the holidays."

"Can we pet them?" asked Sonny.

"They aren't dogs," said Rachel, backing away from an extra-large turkey that was pecking at her shoe. "Shoo!" she said. But the turkey pulled at her shoestring.

16

"He likes you," said Mrs. Atkins, laughing. "He wants to play."

Rachel went to stand by Mrs. Peters. She didn't want to play with a turkey. "Yuck," she said. "They look dirty."

"You'd be dirty too if you lived on a turkey farm," said Roger.

The boys walked into the field of turkeys. Some of the turkeys were as tall as the boys!

"I never saw so many turkeys," said Mary Beth to Molly.

"I never saw *any* turkeys," replied Molly. "Except dead turkeys in the freezer at the grocery store."

Molly and Mary Beth sat on a log at the side of the field and looked at the ocean of white feathers.

"They are so pretty," said Mary Beth. "They aren't dirty. And they look happy."

Molly reached out and patted a large,

friendly turkey on the head. "He's soft!" said Molly. "Soft like a kitten on the top of his head."

"You're right," said Mary Beth. She petted one too.

"I'm going to call that one Fluffy," said Molly. "Here, Fluffy, here, Fluffy!" she called.

"Look! He's coming!" said Mary Beth. "He's really smart."

It looked as if the turkey understood what Molly had said. She patted him on the head again.

"Look!" said Mary Beth. She pointed. "That turkey is after Rachel again."

The same turkey that played with Rachel's shoestring was chasing her around.

"Help!" shouted Rachel, running across the field. "Help!"

Right behind Rachel ran the turkey, gobbling and screeching.

18

Roger and the boys ran to help.

"He doesn't like her," said Lisa with a laugh.

Roger caught the turkey and Rachel ran back to Mrs. Peters.

"I want to sit on the bus," she cried.

"You can come into the house and have some cookies," said Mrs. Atkins.

Rachel looked doubtful.

"She thinks there might be a turkey in the house too," said Lisa.

Suddenly a man in overalls came to feed the turkeys. He threw handfuls of feed out over their heads. They squawked and gobbled and pecked until it was gone. Then the man threw some more.

"Go get it, Fluffy!" said Molly. "Eat your dinner."

"And get fat enough to roast," said Lisa.

Molly felt awful. Lisa was right. The more Fluffy ate, the fatter he got. And the fatter he got, the better he would be to roast for Thanksgiving dinner.

"No one can eat Fluffy," said Molly.

"Or any of them," said Mary Beth. "They are all so soft and friendly."

"Gobble, gobble, gobble," said Roger, running by.

"Squawk, squawk, squawk!" said Sonny, chasing him.

The Pee Wees picked out their favorite turkeys.

Molly's favorite was Fluffy. She followed him around and watched him. She talked to him in turkey sounds.

A big white turkey with two black tail feathers was following Sonny around. Wherever Sonny went, the turkey followed.

The Scouts sat in the warm sun watching the turkeys for a long time. "I like them," said Molly.

"Everyone into the house!" called Mrs. Peters. "For some milk and cookies."

The Scouts filed into Mrs. Atkins's house. Rachel was already there. Molly didn't feel like milk and cookies. She didn't want to eat anything. Even turkey. Especially turkey.

"I want to take my turkey home," said Sonny.

"You'll have a turkey at home," said Roger gloomily. "At Thanksgiving."

"I want a live turkey," said Sonny. "Not a dead turkey."

"Turkeys live on farms," said Mrs. Peters.

Sonny began to cry. "I want him," he said.

Big baby, thought Molly. She would have

said it out loud, but Sonny's mother was there. She didn't want to hurt her feelings. Maybe she felt bad about having such a baby for a son.

"Can I take my turkey home?" pleaded Sonny. "Please?"

The Scouts looked disgusted.

Scouts shouldn't be babies.

Mrs. Betz was very patient with Sonny.

"Where would he live?" asked Mrs. Betz.

"I'll build him a house," said Sonny.

"He'd be lonely," said Mrs. Betz.

"He'd have me," said Sonny. "I'd play with him."

Mrs. Betz shook her head. "I don't know."

"Pleeeease," begged Sonny. He had one knee on the floor now.

Molly was disgusted. Sonny could get a badge for being the biggest baby in Troop 23.

"I suppose it would be a good experience for you," said Mrs. Betz.

A turkey? A good experience? Molly couldn't believe her ears! She wanted to take Fluffy home too, but she would never ask! Her mother would never let her keep a turkey.

Mrs. Betz talked to Mrs. Atkins. Then she paid her some money. Sonny dashed out the door to find the turkey with the two black tail feathers.

"You'll need a gunnysack," said Mrs. Atkins, laughing.

"Not my turkey," said Sonny. "He's not going into a sack."

Mrs. Betz sighed and asked Mrs. Atkins for a rope. Sonny tied it around the turkey's leg.

"Come on, Tiger," he said. "Heel."

CHAPTER 3
Indian or Pilgrim?

"Tiger?" cried Roger. "A turkey named Tiger? Ha!" Roger held his sides, laughing.

Tiger did not want to get on the bus.

Gobble, gobble, gobble.

Squawk, squawk, squawk.

Tiger's wings flapped. He sputtered and fluttered. Feathers flew everywhere. Soon the whole bus was full of feathers.

Mrs. Peters did not look happy. The Pee Wees did not look happy. They did not sing on the way home. They did not laugh.

No one had much to say except Tiger. He sat on the seat next to Sonny with his feathers puffed out.

Molly kept thinking of Fluffy and the other turkeys waiting to go to market. Molly made up her mind she would never eat turkey again. She would choke before she ate Fluffy. She would eat peanut butter instead.

Next Tuesday came quickly. The Pee Wees gathered at Mrs. Peters's house to plan the Thanksgiving play.

"Where is Sonny?" said Mrs. Peters when the Pee Wees got off the bus.

No one knew. "Maybe he forgot that today is Scout day," said Kevin.

"I'll bet he went home to feed his turkey first," said Mary Beth.

Mary Beth was right. Far down the street the Scouts could see Sonny coming. He had a red dog leash in his hand. At the end of the leash was his turkey, Tiger.

"You can't bring a turkey to a Scout meeting!" cried Tim.

"Mrs. Peters, if Sonny can bring his turkey to Scouts, can I bring my cat?" asked Lisa.

Mrs. Peters held up her hand. "No pets allowed," she said firmly. "Except my dog, Tiny, who lives here, and our mascot, Lucky."

"Arf! Arf!" said Tiny.

"Yip! Yip!" said Lucky.

The dogs ran in a circle, Sonny ran toward them with his turkey. Wings flapped and feathers flew. Lots and lots of feathers.

The dogs got very excited.

"You have to take him home," said Rachel. "No pets allowed."

"I'm sorry, Sonny, but you'll have to leave him outside," said Mrs. Peters. She made sure that Lucky and Tiny stayed inside.

"That's all right," said Sonny cheerfully. "Tiger lives outside."

Sonny tied the red leash to a tree in Mrs. Peters's yard. "Good boy," he said to the turkey. "You just lie down and take a nap and wait for me. I'll be out to get you in a little while."

Tiger, the turkey, shook his feathers. "Gobble, gobble," he said.

"After a while I'll show you some tricks he can do," said Sonny. "Hey, can I get a badge for teaching Tiger tricks?" he asked Mrs. Peters.

Mrs. Peters looked doubtful. "I don't think there is a badge for turkey tricks, Sonny."

"The Scout book says there is a badge for building a birdhouse," Sonny went on. "If I build a house for Tiger, can I get that badge?"

"I'll help!" shouted Roger.

"Me too!" said Kevin and Patty.

Mrs. Peters got out the Pee Wee Scout handbook. Sure enough, Sonny was right. There was a badge for building a birdhouse, and a turkey was a bird. The Scouts gathered around Mrs. Peters and looked at the picture.

"It will be a pretty big birdhouse," said Kenny. He laughed. "Too big to hang in a tree."

"It doesn't say it has to be in a tree," said Sonny. "It just says it has to be built for a bird."

"My dad will help us," said Patty.

"Let's start now," said Roger.

"Not now!" said Mrs. Peters. "You will have to work on that badge on Saturday. Today we are going to plan the Thanksgiving play."

The Pee Wees sat in Mrs. Peters's living

room. She told them about the pilgrims and the hard time they had getting food the first winter. She told them about the Indians, and about the first harvest and the first Thanksgiving.

Molly felt like crying, it was so sad. Those poor pilgrims, in a new land without food.

"Why didn't they go to the grocery store and buy food?" asked Tim.

"Dummy," said Tracy. "Where would they get money? There was no money then."

"There were no grocery stores back then!" shouted Roger.

"That's right," said Mrs. Peters. "There was nothing in America then, not even a grocery store."

While the Pee Wees were thinking about those long-ago days, Mrs. Peters passed out papers with the lines in the play.

"Now, we have parts for six pilgrims and five Indians," she said.

"I want to be an Indian!" shouted Roger, waving his hand in the air.

"All right, Roger, you be Indian number one. Now, who wants to be the Indian chief?"

"I do!" shouted Sonny.

Roger frowned. He didn't know there would be a chief.

"All right, Sonny, you be the chief. And Tim and Tracy and Kevin can be the other three Indians."

Now the only thing left is pilgrims, thought Molly.

"The pilgrim mother," said Mrs. Peters. "Molly, will you be the mother?"

Molly didn't want a part at all. She couldn't act like a real actress. She couldn't remember lines. Once in kindergarten she was Little Bo Peep and she couldn't cry.

But there were eleven parts for eleven Scouts. She had to take one.

"All right," said Molly.

Mrs. Peters gave the other pilgrim parts to the rest of the Scouts.

"Now," said Mrs. Peters. "The important thing is to learn your lines. Take the paper home and put an X by the line you have to say. We will practice at the next meeting, and talk about our costumes."

The Scouts said their pledge and sang their song. The meeting was over. When the Scouts came out of the house, Tiger said, "Gobble, gobble."

"Did you hear that?" cried Sonny. "He said my name!"

CHAPTER 4

A Birdhouse for Tiger

On Saturday Mary Beth went over to Molly's house. They studied their parts for the play together.

"I know I won't remember my lines," said Molly.

"It's only one line," said Mary Beth helpfully. "You'll remember. I think I know mine, and it's longer than yours."

The girls pretended Molly's sun porch was a stage.

Mary Beth explained, "When Rachel says 'It's a hard winter, and our food is almost

34

gone,' it is your turn to say your line. I'll be Rachel."

Molly nodded. She felt nervous already.

" 'It's a hard winter, and our food is almost gone,' " said Mary Beth.

Molly's mind went blank.

Blank, blank, blank.

She couldn't think of one word.

"Come on," said Mary Beth. "Say your line."

Molly opened her mouth to talk. She thought maybe her line would come out. But it didn't. Nothing came out. "I can't remember it!" she cried.

"Your line is 'We will pick berries and shoot a wild turkey for dinner,' " said Mary Beth.

Molly and Mary Beth said the lines until they were right.

"But I'll forget it when we are on the stage," said Molly.

"No you won't," said Mary Beth. "I have to go home and take care of my little sister," she added. "Walk halfway with me."

Molly got her jacket and cap and the girls started down the street. The lines from the play were ringing in Molly's head.

"Look!" Mary Beth pointed. "What's going on at Sonny's house?"

Molly looked. In the open garage Sonny and Roger and Patty and Kevin all stood together. Tied outside to a clothespole, on his red leash, was Tiger the turkey.

Sonny waved. "Come and help," he called. "We're building a birdhouse for Tiger."

"We can't stay," said Mary Beth. But the girls walked over to see how the house was coming.

It was just a pile of boards. Old boards. Patty had a long ruler. She was trying to measure Tiger.

"Hold still," she told the turkey. "Can you hold him?" she asked the girls.

It took both girls, plus Kevin and Roger and Sonny, to hold Tiger. Patty held up the ruler. Tiger didn't want to be measured. He jumped around.

Finally Patty said, "He is as tall as three rulers."

"Three feet tall," said Roger.

"He needs more room than that in his house," said Sonny. "He needs room to move around."

"Four feet," said Roger.

Roger and Sonny and Kevin marked the boards. They read the directions out loud.

"I think you should get directions for a doghouse," said Molly. "That would be more his size."

"There's no badge for building a doghouse," said Sonny. "It has to be a birdhouse. Anyway, Tiger's a bird, not a dog."

Patty was sawing the places where Roger had measured. It took a long time with Sonny's toy saw. Soon Patty was out of breath. "We better take it to my house so my dad can help," she said.

The girls waved good-bye.

"You'll see his house on Tuesday," called Sonny.

On Tuesday, Sonny and Roger and Kevin were late for the Pee Wee Scout meeting. The rest of the Pee Wees were making some old hats into pilgrim hats.

Suddenly there was a terrible racket outside.

A dragging sound.

A scraping sound.

Drag, scrape, bump, crash!

Mrs. Peters ran to the door.

Tiger was tied to the tree. The boys were

dragging the birdhouse up Mrs. Peters's steps.

"Maybe we should look at it outside," said Mrs. Peters. "It's too big to bring inside."

The Pee Wees ran outside to see the birdhouse. It was huge! Big enough for Tiny! He was a Labrador, a large dog.

The birdhouse had one crooked window with no glass in it.

"That's for fresh air," said Sonny.

The roof was flat. Some shingles were nailed to the top.

"The door's too little," said Molly. "Only a robin would fit through there."

"It doesn't have to be perfect," said Sonny crossly.

"We forgot to change the directions for the door," admitted Patty. "But we made the rest bigger."

"It's a wonderful birdhouse," said Mrs.

Peters. "You all have worked very hard and you deserve the badge. We will give these badges out at the town hall after the play. When the parents are there to see you."

"Does Tiger like his house?" asked Tim.

"He can't get through the door," said Sonny sadly.

"Ho!" Rachel laughed. "What good is it if he can't get in?"

"He sits on top," said Sonny. "And when it gets cold we are going to make the door bigger."

The Pee Wees went back into Mrs. Peters's house. They finished making their pilgrim hats.

"We'll just wear bathrobes for the pilgrim dresses," said Mrs. Peters. "Unless your mother has time to make you a dress. And the Indians can just wear blue jeans, but they will have Indian headbands with feathers."

"I can get feathers!" shouted Sonny.

"That would be fine, Sonny. We will dye them different colors and some of the mothers will sew them onto headbands."

Sonny smiled.

"Now let's go through our play," said Mrs. Peters.

The pilgrims put their hats on. The Indians pretended they had feathers. Everyone stood in a row in Mrs. Peters's living room.

Molly was already nervous. "I can't act," she said. "I can't remember my line."

"I never get nervous," boasted Rachel. "I'm used to being onstage dancing and twirling my baton."

Rat's knees, thought Molly. Why did I say I couldn't act? Rachel will find out soon enough.

" 'It's a hard winter, and our food is almost gone,' " said Rachel. She spoke her line clearly.

Mary Beth jabbed Molly in the back. "Say it," she whispered.

But Molly's mind was blank again. Blank, blank, blank. All she could think of was how nervous she felt.

" 'We will pick—' " Mary Beth prompted.

Molly remembered! "We will pick wild turkeys and shoot a wild berry!" She blurted out the line.

All of the Pee Wees roared with laughter. Even Molly's best friend, Mary Beth.

Roger jumped up and began to run around. He pretended to have an imaginary shotgun. "Shoot a berry!" he cried. "Ho, ho, pick a turkey!" Roger laughed the loudest.

Mrs. Peters put her arm around Molly. "You just got a little nervous," she said. "You go over your line before the play. You will do fine."

But Molly knew she wouldn't do fine.

Oh, no. I can't act at all, she thought. I'll ruin the play!

At the end of the meeting, the Scouts told about some good deeds they had done. Then Mrs. Peters led them as they said the Pee Wee Scout pledge and sang the Pee Wee Scout song.

Sometimes, thought Molly, it was no fun to be a Pee Wee Scout.

No fun at all.

CHAPTER 5
Back to the Farm

Thanksgiving got closer and closer. The play got closer and closer too. It would be on the day before Thanksgiving.

Molly practiced her line with Mary Beth. She knew it perfectly. But when she thought of the stage at the town hall, her stomach felt like Jell-O. She was sure she would forget what to say.

The Thanksgiving baskets were filled and ready. On the Saturday before Thanksgiving, the Pee Wees came to Mrs. Peters's

46

house. Mr. Peters would take the baskets to the volunteer center. The Pee Wees helped load them into the car.

"Here's mine!" shouted Sonny.

"There's Rachel's," said Lisa. "It's shorter than the others."

"Tall or short, the people will be glad to get them," said Mrs. Peters.

Mr. Peters drove away with the baskets.

Sonny had Tiger on his leash. "Do you want to see him do his tricks?" asked Sonny.

"Ha," said Kenny. "I'll bet he can't do much."

"Sit up!" said Sonny to the turkey. He held a cookie in his hand over the turkey's head.

Peck, peck, peck went Tiger. He checked the ground for food.

"Here, boy, up here," said Sonny.

Some of the Pee Wees covered their faces.

They were laughing. They didn't want
Sonny to see.

Sonny took a cracker out of his pocket.
He held it up. Just when Tiger was ready
to peck at it, Sonny raised it higher. The

turkey stretched his neck and grabbed the cracker.

"See? See? Did you see him sit up?" shouted Sonny.

"He didn't sit up," said Tracy. "He just stretched his neck."

"He sat up," insisted Sonny. "Now watch this."

Sonny held up another cracker. "Speak!" said Sonny. "Come on, speak, boy!"

The turkey stopped pecking the ground. He looked at the cracker out of one eye. "Gobble, gobble," he said.

"I told you! I told you!" shouted Sonny, patting Tiger on his head.

"He's been gobbling all along," said Rachel. "Turkeys gobble all the time."

But Sonny didn't answer. He was trying to get Tiger to roll over and play dead.

"I have to go home and practice the piano," said Rachel.

The rest of the Pee Wees had to leave too. Except Mrs. Peters. She couldn't leave. It was her house.

"He did it yesterday," said Sonny. "Roll over, boy."

Finally Sonny had to give Tiger a shove and roll him over.

"He's a smart turkey," said Mrs. Peters, going into the house.

The next Tuesday, the Pee Wees had their last Scout meeting before Thanksgiving. They practiced their play. They put the final touches on their costumes.

The Indians tried on their headbands with Tiger's colored feathers. Roger pretended to shoot a bow and arrow.

"These are friendly Indians," called Mrs. Peters. "They smoke a peace pipe and try to help the pilgrims."

"I wonder where Sonny is," whispered Mary Beth to Molly. "He is never this late for Scouts."

Just as the Pee Wee Scouts were finishing their cocoa and cookies, Sonny burst in the door. Tears were streaming down his face. He was crying out loud.

"Sonny, what happened?" asked Mrs. Peters, putting her arms around him. "Are you hurt?"

Sonny sniffed and wiped his nose on his sleeve. "It's Tiger," he cried. When he said the turkey's name, Sonny began to sob all over again.

"Did he get hit by a car?" asked Tim.

"Is he dead?" said Roger.

"He—he—" Sonny just couldn't finish his sentence. He sniffled and tried again, "He has to go back to the turkey farm," he said. "My mom says our house is no place for a turkey. She said he misses his friends.

And besides, the neighbors complained about his gobbling!"

Even Molly felt like crying now. It was awful to lose a pet. Poor Sonny!

The Scouts all looked sad about Tiger. Still, thought Molly, Mrs. Betz should have known better than to give in to Sonny.

"I am sure you can go and visit him," said Mrs. Peters. "And you will like to see him back with his friends."

Sonny nodded. But he was still crying. The Scouts could hear Tiger gobbling outside under the tree.

"When is he going?" asked Patty.

"When I get home," said Sonny. He sniffled.

"Maybe we could all ride along," said Mrs. Peters. "And have kind of a send-off for Tiger."

Sonny's eyes lit up. "Really?" Sonny loved a party.

"I'll call your mom," said Mrs. Peters.

Mrs. Betz said yes.

The Scouts called home to be sure they could go along to say good-bye to Tiger. Then they all piled into two cars. Mrs. Peters drove and Mrs. Betz drove. Tiger flapped and gobbled and pecked on Sonny's lap. Sonny hugged him tight.

"He lost his two black tail feathers," Molly noticed.

"From all that flapping," said Mary Beth. The girls laughed.

When the Scouts got to the turkey farm, they marched out to the turkey field. Then Mrs. Peters gave a short speech about how lucky Tiger was to be with his friends. "He has lots to be thankful for this Thanksgiving Day," she said.

"Yeah, the roasting pan," snickered Roger.

Molly turned around and glared at Roger. "Shhh," she said loudly. Sonny would start

to cry all over again if he thought that Tiger would be someone's dinner.

"All right," said Mrs. Betz. "Let him go, Sonny."

It reminded Molly of a TV show where they released an eagle with a mended wing.

Sonny didn't let go. Mrs. Betz gave the bird a push. Off he went into the crowd of turkeys.

"You can come and see him anytime," said Mrs. Atkins.

As the Scouts said good-bye and walked back to the cars, Kevin said something. Something Molly had been thinking about all along.

"He can't visit Tiger," said Kevin. "He won't know which turkey is Tiger. He looks just like all those other turkeys out there!"

It was true. Tiger was just part of the ocean of white feathers. Peck, peck. Gobble,

gobble. Any one of those turkeys could be Tiger.

Then Kevin said, "I'm not eating any turkey on Thanksgiving."

"Neither am I," said Sonny with a sniffle.

"I'm eating peanut butter instead," said Molly. "I'm going to ask my mom."

"No turkey, no turkey," chanted the Scouts as they climbed back into the cars and went home.

6

Molly Saves the Day

Soon it was the day before the Thanksgiving play. The Pee Wees and their dads were busy at the town hall.

They painted the scenery.

They set up chairs for the audience.

Mrs. Betz climbed up high on a ladder to paint the sky. Sonny didn't have a dad, so his mom came instead. "Hand me that big brush, son," she called down to Sonny.

Mr. Peters and Mr. Duff were setting up cornstalks at the sides of the stage.

Mary Beth's dad and the twins' dad were fixing the lights.

Molly tried to imagine how she would feel when there were people in those chairs. When she was standing under those lights. Under Mrs. Betz's blue sky. Oh! Would she remember her line?

"Now, all the Pee Wees not working come over to this table and color these turkeys," said Mrs. Peters. "We need lots of turkeys for the background."

"For the first Thanksgiving dinner," said Kevin's dad.

The Pee Wees didn't like to think of eating turkey. Molly was glad these turkeys were cardboard.

"Tiger could be in this play," said Sonny. "He could be an actor."

"A cardboard turkey may be a better actor than a live turkey," said Mrs. Peters, laughing.

58

Molly knew Mrs. Peters was right. A real turkey would squawk and flap and gobble. He would probably run off the stage and out the back door!

The Pee Wees worked very hard. They colored all the turkeys and set them up at one side of the stage. One turkey had two black tail feathers.

"How about the berry bushes?" said Roger. "So Molly can shoot a berry for dinner?"

Molly wanted to punch Roger. She felt bad enough about mixing up her line. Roger wouldn't let anyone forget a mistake.

"Pick a turkey, shoot a berry!" sang Roger. Some of the other boys joined in. "Pick a turkey, shoot a berry!"

Mrs. Peters held up her hand for quiet. "We'll just have to pretend there are bushes," she said.

Finally all the work was done.

The turkeys.

The lights.

The chairs.

The scenery.

"Now we just wait until tomorrow night!" said Mr. White. He sounds just like Roger, thought Molly. He even looks like Roger!

The dads took down the ladders. They put the paint away. Then everyone began to leave.

"Do you think a lot of people will come to the play?" Molly asked Mary Beth.

"I hope so," said Mary Beth.

"My dad knows the mayor," said Rachel. "And he might come to the play, my dad says."

"That's true," said Mrs. Peters. "The mayor is coming."

Now Molly was really nervous. The mayor of their town! At a Pee Wee Scout play! She could mess up the whole play by forgetting her line. She could ruin Thanksgiving! Everyone would point to her on the street and say, "She's the one who messed up the play in front of the mayor!"

"All my aunts are coming," said Lisa. "And my grandma."

"My cousin is coming from California," said Kevin.

"All that way, just for the play?" said Lisa.

"Well, he's coming for Thanksgiving," Kevin admitted.

The Pee Wee Scouts waved to one another and went home. They needed a good night's sleep before the play.

All night long Molly had bad dreams. She dreamed her mouth was frozen shut. She tried to speak and she couldn't. The mayor sat in the front seat and laughed and laughed.

Molly was shaking when she woke up. "I hope that doesn't happen," she said out loud.

All morning Molly said her line over and over. " 'We will pick berries and shoot a wild turkey for dinner.' "

During breakfast, she said it.

On the way to the store, she said it.

At lunch, she said it.

Molly's mom was making the stuffing for their turkey. Molly didn't want to look in the refrigerator. The naked dead turkey was in there. The turkey with all its soft feathers gone.

"Do I have to eat turkey?" asked Molly.

Molly's mother knew about the trip to the turkey farm. "Of course not," said Mrs. Duff. "But what will you eat instead?"

"Peanut butter," said Molly quickly. "And dressing and gravy and cranberries and pumpkin pie."

Mrs. Duff laughed. "You'll be the first pilgrim to eat peanut butter," she said.

But not the only one, thought Molly. She felt relieved. She just couldn't eat any relative of Tiger's or Fluffy's.

The rest of Molly's day flew by. Soon it was time to take her bath and get into her costume. It was dark outside, and beginning to snow.

All the Pee Wee Scouts were meeting at the town hall at six-thirty. In the car, Molly said her line over and over. She didn't see how she could possibly forget it. No matter how nervous she was!

The Pee Wees were all on time.

The Indians and pilgrims whispered to one another behind the curtain.

Molly pulled the curtain aside to look out at the audience. The town hall was almost filled! She saw her second-grade teacher in the third row.

"Molly peeked," whispered Rachel to Mrs. Peters.

But Mrs. Peters didn't mind.

Rachel had makeup on. Pilgrim makeup.

"Pilgrims don't wear lipstick," said Mary Beth.

"Everyone knows you need makeup on-stage," Rachel answered. "So people can see you from the back of the room."

"Do not," said Lisa.

"Do too," said Rachel.

"Either way is all right," said Mrs. Peters.

That meant there was nothing to fight about. Mrs. Peters is smart, thought Molly. She never takes sides.

Mrs. Peters straightened the Indian head-bands. And the pilgrim hats. Some lively music started. Mrs. Betz was playing the piano in the back of the room. Soon it would be time for the curtain to go up!

Molly took one more little peek into the

audience. There he was! In the front row. Mr. Green, the mayor.

"Look!" said Molly, pointing. "The mayor is here!"

But it was too late to worry. It was time to begin. Molly waited backstage until it was her turn to go on the stage.

She could have said her line in her sleep. She was already sick of it. Boring. Snoring, boring. It was easy now. She whispered it again to herself, just to be sure.

She heard Roger say his line, and Lisa, and then she and Rachel walked onto the stage.

Molly blinked at the bright lights. She could see people in front of her. A whole hall full of people! Some were even standing in the back. And right in the front row, looking at her, was the mayor.

Molly waited for Rachel to say her line, so she could say hers.

She waited.

And waited.

What was wrong? Why wasn't Rachel talking?

Molly looked at her.

Rachel had turned white. Her lipstick was

bright red on her white face. "I forgot my line!" she whispered.

Molly couldn't believe it.

But she knew Rachel's line. She knew everyone's lines by now. She had read the play over and over so many times.

" 'It's a hard winter and our food is almost gone,' " whispered Molly. She hoped it was loud enough for Rachel to hear. And quiet enough so no one else would hear.

Rachel looked relieved. Her face got pink again. "It's a hard winter, and we have no food," she said loudly.

The audience tittered. Then they clapped.

Now it was Molly's turn. " 'We will pick berries and shoot a wild turkey for dinner,' " said Molly. Loud and clear. She would never forget that line again. Never in her whole life!

The rest of the play went on. Sonny was a funny Indian chief. All the Pee Wees said their lines.

Molly tried to look like a hungry pilgrim.

A hardworking pilgrim.

A brave pilgrim.

It was fun to act! Maybe she would be a movie star when she grew up.

Then it was all over. Too soon. Molly wanted it to go on and on.

The curtain closed, and then it opened again. The Pee Wee Scouts came out on the stage and bowed. All the people in the town hall clapped and clapped.

Then the mayor got up and walked right onto the stage! He said what fine actors the Pee Wee Scouts were and thanked them for all the good deeds they did for the community.

"The Thanksgiving baskets made some families very happy," he said. "Now, I understand there are some badges to be given out."

Mrs. Peters came out with the badges, and the list of names.

The mayor gave out their badges. One by one he called their names. Everyone got a playacting badge. And everyone got a pilgrim-Indian badge too.

Then Roger, Sonny, Patty, and Kevin got badges for building the birdhouse.

Mrs. Peters smiled. She was proud of her Pee Wee Scouts.

Everyone clapped loudly all over again. Mrs. Betz played "America the Beautiful" on the piano, and everybody sang. Then they went downstairs for coffee and cookies.

"You remembered your line!" said Mary Beth to Molly. "And Rachel's too!"

Rachel looked sheepish.

"Well, anyone can forget," said Molly. Then she added, "Guess what, my mom said I could eat peanut butter on Thanksgiving instead of turkey!"

"Mine did too," said Mary Beth. "She said there would be plenty of people to eat the turkey."

The mayor was drinking coffee. And shaking hands. When he shook Kevin's hand, the Scouts heard Kevin say, "I'm going to be mayor when I grow up."

"Well, I'm glad my term will be over by then," said the mayor with a laugh. "Otherwise I'd have to worry about my job!"

The Scouts snickered. It was just like Kevin to want to be mayor. He probably even wants to be president someday, thought Molly.

When everyone was leaving, Mrs. Peters walked up to Molly. "What a wonderful thing you did," she said, "helping Rachel with her line. You saved the day."

"She saved the play," said Roger. "The day and the play."

"Anyone can forget," said Molly.

She was just glad that Thanksgiving was almost over.

Christmas would be here soon!

Pee Wee Scout Song

(to the tune of
"Old MacDonald Had a Farm")

Scouts are helpers, Scouts have fun,
Pee Wee, Pee Wee Scouts!
We sing and play when work is done,
Pee Wee, Pee Wee Scouts!

With a good deed here,
And an errand there,
Here a hand, there a hand,
Everywhere a good hand.

Scouts are helpers, Scouts have fun,
Pee Wee, Pee Wee Scouts!

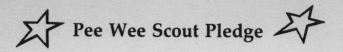 **Pee Wee Scout Pledge**

We love our country
And our home,
Our school and neighbors too.

As Pee Wee Scouts
We pledge our best
In everything we do.